Brockworth
Community Project

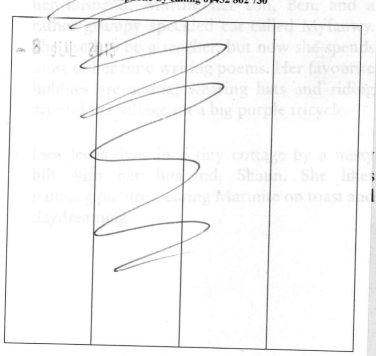

- 8 JUL 2019

D0774499

Also by Clare Bevan and Lara Jones

Fairy Poems
More Fairy Poems
Mermaid Poems
Ballerina Poems

Fairytale Poems

By **Clare Bevan**

Illustrated by **Lara Jones**

MACMILLAN CHILDREN'S BOOKS

First published 2009 by Macmillan Children's Books
a division of Macmillan Publishers Limited
20 New Wharf Road, London N1 9RR
Basingstoke and Oxford
Associated companies throughout the world
www.panmacmillan.com

ISBN 978-0-330-46413-0

3 5 7 9 8 6 4 2

A CIP catalogue record for this book is available from
the British Library.

Printed and bound in the UK by CPI Mackays, Chatham ME5 8TD

For Jack, Eddie and Max.
May your lives be filled with magic.
Also for Rachel, who waved the sparkly wand.

With thanks to the Brothers Grimm, Charles Perrault,
Hans Andersen and all those wonderful storytellers
whose names have been lost in the misty woods.
Thank you for making the world a more magical place.

Contents

Contents

Rapunzel's Poem

Even if a wicked witch trapped me in her tower, I wouldn't want a prince to use my long hair for a ladder – would you?

Pin it or
Plait it or
Tie it in bunches,
Frizzle it,
Twizzle it,
Pop it in scrunchies.

Curl it or
Twirl it or
Fix it in a bun,
Streak it or
Tweak it or
Crimp it for fun.

Braid it,
Rapunzel
And try not to wince . . .
Tangle it,
Dangle it,
HERE COMES A PRINCE.

Rules for Children (and Animals) Who Wander Through the Wild Woods

Actually, the BEST rule is: never wander through the Wild Woods.

1. Don't drop breadcrumbs.
   Birds will eat them.

2. Don't fight dragons.
   Smile and greet them.

3. Don't be nosy. Don't be bold.
   Don't taste porridge, hot or cold.

4. Don't test wooden beds and chairs.
   (If you do, look out for bears.)

5. Don't trust wolves. They're bad.
   They're big.
   They are not safe for girl or pig.

6. If you're hiding from the Queen,
    In a house that's small and green,
    Lock the door and do not buy
    Poisoned apples – you could DIE!

7. Do not climb enchanted trees,
    Twisty stairways tempt and tease . . .
    Children climb them just for fun,
    Then they VANISH, one by one.

8. Do not fall down magic wells –
    Most are full of froggy spells.

9. Even if you've not been fed,
    Don't munch walls of gingerbread –
    Sugar bricks are nice to chew
    But witches can be BAD for you.

10. If a troll says, "Come to tea,"
    Then he eats you – DON'T BLAME
    ME.

The Rickety-rackety Rhyme

*The Three Billy Goats Gruff don't seem very
scared of the Troll. Do you think he'll wake up
and catch them? And do you think the grass really
IS greener on the other side of the bridge?*

Rickety-rackety
Over the bridge –
Silly old Troll,
He can't catch a midge,
He can't catch a measle,
He can't catch a flea,
And he can't catch the Billy Goats
One, Two and Three.

Rickety-rackety
Over we pass,
Looking for greener
And tastier grass.
Silly old Troll,
He makes a big fuss,
But he can't catch a cold
So he'll never catch us.

4

Rickety-rackety,
Over we run,
Teasing the Troll
Is our ONE bit of fun –
Grass is so BORING
It all tastes the same . . .
And THAT'S why we're playing
Our rackety game!

The Trip-trap-troll Rap

I wonder why the sleepy Troll chooses to live under Rickety-rackety Bridge . . .

Don't go trip-trap
Trip-trap tapping –
I'm a Troll who's
Fond of NAPPING!

Goats who wake me
Make me grumpy,
Make my fists go
Thump-thump-thumpy.
I will biff and bash
And beat you,
When I'm finished
I will eat you –

DON'T go trip-trap
Trip-trap tapping,
I'm a Troll whose
Fangs are SNAPPING!

Seven in One Go

In the story, the hero is a poor tailor – and even though he isn't a good fighter, he's very good at teasing giants.

Here is the hero
Who killed (as you know)
Seven cruel creatures
And all in one go!

Did he swipe monsters
With swivelly eyes?
Did he slay dragons
Who sizzle the skies?
Did he biff ogres?
Or take by surprise
The terrible trolls?
Well, I'll tell you no lies . . .

He famously, fearlessly
Squashed SEVEN FLIES!

Shopping List for a Perfect Fairytale

This list was found in a sooty, old book, hidden up a tall chimney.

These are the things a fairytale needs:

> A shivery spell;
> A path that leads
> A princess past
> A spooky wood;
> A wizard (wise);
> A fairy (good);
> A ragged child;
> A dragon (kind);
> A silver thread
> To weave and wind
> Around an ancient
> Treasure box;
> A flying horse;
> A talking fox;
> A castle and
> An empty throne;

A witch who rides
Alone, alone;
A looking glass
In need of mending,
And (most of all)
A Happy Ending.

Snow White's Favourite Sums

Perhaps I would be better at sums if I lived with the Seven Dwarfs.

Snow White was SO good at her seven
    times table –
She counted the Dwarfs any time she was
    able.

She counted the slippers that stood by
    their beds,
She counted their gloves, and the hats for
    their heads.

She counted their cups and their spoons
    and their forks,
She counted their wellies they wore on
    their walks.

She could tell you the answer to seven
    times five,
But she wasn't as clever at staying alive!

So when dear old Dopey said, "Please
    lock the door,"
All she could think of was seven times
    four . . .

Now – I know it's quite classy to add and
    to double,
But you STILL need to learn that a witch
    equals trouble.

Some Fairytale Jokes

The Three Little Pigs, the Three Billy Goats and the Three Bears love to tell jokes – especially ones about the Big Bad Wolf!

What did the Witch say when her
    Gingerbread House fell to bits?
Crumbs!

What did the First Little Pig say when his
    Straw House blew down?
Hay!

What do you call a goat who teases a
   very tired troll?
Silly Billy.

What do you call a troll with a frog
   sleeping in each ear?
Anything you like – he can't hear you!

What did Jack's mum say when he came
   home from the market?
Where have you BEAN?

What did Puss in Boots say when his new
   boots were too tight?
Mia-OWWWW!

What did the Frog Prince say when the
   Princess gave him a storybook?
Reddit! Reddit!

What did the Big Bad Wolf do when
   Granny beat him in the marathon?
He huffed and he puffed, of course.

And why did Cinderella ask her little dog
   to wag his tail?
*Because everyone loves a HAPPY
   ENDING!*

13

A Wisdom of Wizards

If you like collecting things, you'll want ALL these special words.

A Smoulder of Dragons;
A Fanfare of Kings;
A Flutter of Horses
With feathery wings;
A Gallop of Princes;
A Sleep of Princesses;
A Curtsy of Queens
In their rustly dresses;
A Tumble of Ogres;
A Grumble of Frogs;
A Huffing of Wolves
And a Dribble of Dogs.

A Bristle of Broomsticks;
A Dangle of Bats;
A Bubble of Cauldrons;
A Yowling of Cats;
A Wisdom of Wizards;
A Crackle of Spells;
A Dazzle of Treasure
In caverns and wells;
A Ripple of Carpets
To skim over sands;
A Scribble of Pathways
Through magical lands.

A Shudder of Shadows;
A Flicker of Lights,
And a Murmur of Stories
On long winter nights.

The Three Princes

There ALWAYS seems to be THREE Princes!

The First-born Prince was a hero, of
    course,
With his glittering sword and his
    galloping horse.
He would rescue the Princess with skill
    and with force . . .
But he vanished like frost in the firelight.

The Middle Prince was a mischievous
    child,
With his armour of gold and his hair
    tangled wild.
He would sneak through the cave where
    the treasure was piled . . .
But he trembled like mice in the
    moonlight.

The Youngest Prince was no more than a
    boy,
With his bag full of bread and his heart
    full of joy.
He would talk to the beast he was sent to
    destroy –
And return like a King in the starlight.

The Three Princesses

*If there are THREE Princes – there must be
THREE Princesses too!*

I'm the Shouty-pouty Princess –
I am bossy to the bone,
I am here to give the orders
In a rude and royal tone.

I'm the Silly-frilly Princess –
I'm the one who likes to moan,
I am always buying dresses
All for me, and all my own.

I'm the Frisky-risky Princess –
I'm the one who walks alone,
I am off to scare the Dragon,
I shall turn her into stone . . .

Then I'll grab her golden treasure
And I'll gain a royal throne.

How to Bake a Delicious House

This recipe can be very hard to find, as it is usually written on paper spun from strawberry-flavoured sugar.

Measure the sugar and
Sprinkle the spice,
Pour in the custard
And coconut ice,
Mix it all up with
A turnabout spoon
Sharp as a bramble
And cold as the moon.
Add a small rainbow,
Say one magic word,
Heat with the flames
Of a fiery bird . . .

Slice up your sweets
With a dragon-child's tooth . . .
Gingerbread bricks for
The walls and the roof,
A lollipop chimney and
Marshmallow stairs,
Jelly for windows and
Chocolate chairs,
Bagfuls of cake-crumbs
To carpet the floors,
Marzipan tables and
Honeycomb doors . . .

Candyfloss flowers on
Sticks tall and straight,
Plus a peppermint path
To the liquorice gate.
(PS I must mention
Some handy advice –
Don't kidnap children
Who nibble like mice,
And DON'T try to cook them . . .
You WON'T try it twice!)

Bad Behaviour

I'm sure YOU would never behave as badly as this . . .

Hansel and Gretel! Just WHAT were you
    thinking?
Merrily munching and greedily drinking
Gingerbread rooftops and lemonade
    lakes?
Windows of jelly and steps carved from
    cakes?
Sugary statues and minty-green moss?
No wonder the Witch was a teeny bit
    cross!

No wonder she said you were mean and
    unkind.
She was PROUD of her home. It was
    neatly designed.
No wonder she wanted to give you a
    fright –
Nibbling houses can NEVER be right.
And though you may say she was wicked
    and warty,
Baking old ladies is TERRIBLY naughty!

The Wicked Witch's Song

If you ever hear a crackly voice singing this song – RUN!

I'm making witch spells,
Give-you-all-an-itch spells,
Stir the steamy cauldron with a monster
    bone,
I'm making mean spells,
Slithery and green spells,
Turn you into lizards on a slimy stone.

I'm making cat spells,
Dangle-like-a-bat spells,
Swish you on a broomstick through the
    inky sky,
I'm making shark spells,
Dangerous and dark spells,
Give you all a nightmare till you scream
    and cry.

A Lullaby for Baby Bear

*If someone squashed MY favourite chair, I would
be upset too.*

Sleep, little bear cub,
Sleep, Baby Bear.
Don't dream of SOMEONE
With long, curly hair,
Who ate all your porridge,
Who broke your best chair,
Who naughtily, naughtily
Stamped up the stair.

Sleep, little bear cub,
Sleep, Baby Ted.
Don't dream of SOMEONE
Who borrowed your bed,
Who crumpled your pillow,
Who left a gold thread,
Who naughtily, naughtily
Screamed as she fled.

Sleep, little bear cub,
Sleep through the night.
Don't dream of SOMEONE
Who gave you a fright,
Who tripped on your slippers,
Who tangled your kite,
Who naughtily, naughtily
Vanished from sight.

Sleep, little bear cub,
Sleep until day.
Dream about SOMEONE
Who visits to say
She's terribly sorry,
She's willing to pay . . .
Then nervously, nervously
Scampers away.

Oh My Goodness!

It's the Sleeping Beauty Story.

Oh my goodness! How the Fairy
(Aunty Angry) stamped and shrieked.
How her twisty wand went waving,
How her pointy slippers creaked.

How she cursed the royal baby,
How her words rang round the throne:
"How I hate you! How I'll hurt you
With a spindle, when you're grown."

How the King began to panic,
How the Queen began to weep,
How the Fairy (Cousin Kindly) said,
"She shall not die. She'll sleep."

How the birthdays whizzed like
    whirlwinds,
How the Princess grew and grew,
How the worried servants wondered,
"Will the wicked spell come true?"

How the stairway whispered, "Climb me."
How the doorway squeaked, "Come in."
How the shadows hissed, "Be careful."
How the wooden wheel said, "SPIN!"

How the drop of blood hung brightly,
How the girl fell to the floor,
How the spiders wrapped her gently,
How the castle seemed to snore.

How the brambles clawed and clambered,
How the years crept by like snails,
How the Prince (at last) came striding
Down the spooky, spiky trails.

How he drew the dusty curtains,
How the magic snapped in two,
How the Princess cried, "My goodness!
How I've dreamed of meeting YOU."

27

Who Am I?

*There is a name hidden in this poem somewhere –
can YOU find it?*

Am I a thief, with a
Lamp from a cave?
Am I a poor boy who
Dares to be brave?
Do I win love and a genie and fame
Inside a palace where magic's a game?
Nod if you think you've discovered my
     name.

* *

*Answer: Did you search both up and down?
I'm ALADDIN – Prince and Clown.*

New Lamps for Old

This is the wicked magician's song. If you ever meet him, DON'T give him any old lamps. They might be more precious than you think.

New lamps for old!
New lamps for old!
Choose from the silver,
The green or the gold.
Small ones or tall ones
With handles that curl,
Prim ones with patterns
That zigzag or twirl.
Wide ones or slim ones,
The bulgy, the bold,
Choose one and lose one . . .
NEW LAMPS FOR OLD!

Old lamps for new!
Old lamps for new!
One will be hiding
A genie or two.
Soon I'll have treasure
And sugary cakes,
Castles that fly
Over forests and lakes,
Soon all my greediest
Dreams will come true,
Lose one and choose one . . .
OLD LAMPS FOR NEW!

The Very Lonely Genie

I'd love to find this magic bottle, wouldn't you?
And I know EXACTLY what my first wish would
be.

There's a genie in a bottle,
But the bottle's very small,
And the genie's very bulgy,
Very strong and very tall.

So he isn't very happy,
Since it's such an awful squash,
And he's very bored and lonely,
And he longs to have a wash.

If you saw that little bottle
(In a shed? A cave? a ditch?)
You could open up the stopper
And he'd make you VERY rich.

He would let you ride a camel,
Or a carpet for a day,
You could own a magic castle
On an island far away.

But he sobs inside his bottle
(By a lake? A rock? A tree?)
"I would grant a thousand wishes,
But there's only one for me."

When you find him,
IF you find him,
Could you kindly set him free?

Aladdin's Flying Carpet

Do you wish YOU could sail away on a magic carpet? I do!

Sail over palm trees

Soar over sands

Race with the dragons

To faraway lands,

Ripple like water,

Flap like the birds,

Swoop when I whisper

Your magical words.

33

Name That Dragon

If I could have a tiny dragon, I would call it Sparks.

Dragons have the OLDEST names,
Dark as danger, fierce as flames.

Golden-fang or Spiny-tail,
Fury, Roary, Rattle-scale,

Sky-lord, Grabber, Princess-catcher,
Shadow-lady, Hero-snatcher,

Thunder-tooth or Smoky-jaw,
Smoulder, Scorch or Cinder-claw,

Leather-wing or Sorrow-maker,
Cavern-king or Treasure-taker,

Battle-queen or Mighty-biter,
Sword-snap, Bone-crunch, Fiery-fighter.

Dragon names are secret things,
Wild as weather, swift as stings.

What Am I?

Can you guess who is teasing you before you reach the answer?

I'm a . . .

Fear-Bringing,

Weird-Singing,

Sword-Breaking,

Treasure-Taking,

Cave-Sleeping,

Crown-Keeping,

Sky-Shaking,

Smoke-Making,

Fire-Sneezing,

Castle-Teasing,

Prince-Beating,

King-Defeating,

Princess-Eating . . .

DRAGON!!

Dragon Tale

Have you ever wondered if the Princess felt sorry for the fiery Dragon?

Well, the Prince looked at the Princess
And the Princess looked at him,
Then they both looked at the Dragon
(Who was green and grey and grim)
And the Dragon stretched his wing-flaps
As he sang his mournful hymn . . .

"Oh, who will save my treasure chest
And who will wear my crown
And who will guard my Princess
In her wispy, silver gown,
When the hero from the castle
Chains me up and knocks me down?"

Well, the Prince looked at the Princess
And she shuddered with regret,
Then they both looked at the Dragon
Who was grey and grim – and yet
He was very small and lonely . . .
So they kept him as a pet.

37

Beauty's Song

Beauty likes to sing this song when she dances
with her Beast-prince.

How I feared him,
How I feared him,
Though his eyes were rather sad,
Though his house was rather homely,
Though his garden made me glad.

How I liked him,
How I liked him,
Though his face was rather long,
Rather scruffy, rather scary,
Rather hairy like King Kong.

How I missed him,
How I missed him,
When I left him for a while,
Though his fangs were rather fearsome,
And he wore a spooky smile.

How I hugged him,
How I hugged him,
Though my heart felt rather strange . . .
Then my Beast grew rather handsome,
Though he didn't really change.

He is just as kind as ever,
Rather frisky, rather fun
How I love him,
How he loves me,
Though our fairytale is done.

Pea Poem

The best way to find out if someone is a REAL princess is to pop a tiny dried pea underneath her mattress . . .

I'm only a pea
Who was picked from my pod.
They dipped me and dried me,
Which felt a bit odd.

I'm hard as a conker,
I'm crinkled and green,
They tuck me away
Where I'll never be seen.
I lurk under mattresses –
Two, three or four,
Or maybe a hundred,
Or maybe some more,
And then when a stranger
Arrives from the West
And says she's a princess,
They set her a TEST!

They take her upstairs
To my home in the loft,
They say, "Here's a bed
That's incredibly soft."
Then, if the girl's fibbing,
She'll sleep night and day,
And they'll send her back home
To a land far away.
But if the girl's truthful,
I'll keep her awake,
I'll bump her and bruise her,
She'll groan and she'll ache.
She'll yawn half the morning
In pain and distress,
And the people will yell,
"YOU'RE A PROPER PRINCESS!"

So this is my poem –
I'm only a pea,
But you'll not spot a princess
Without help from ME.

The Emperor's New Clothes

*Here is a very foolish emperor – would YOU dare
to tell him the truth?*

The naughtiest story ever told
Is this one – and it's very old.

An emperor
From long ago
Believed he'd bought
A suit – but no!
Those magic clothes,
So light and rare,
Were made from nothing
But FRESH AIR!

He paid with jewels
From his box . . .
And then put on
His magic socks,
His magic trousers,
Magic coat,
With magic ruffles
Round his throat,
Plus magic shirt
And magic tie . . .
"The best," he thought,
"That gold can buy!"

He swished the robes
He couldn't see,
He checked his mirror,
Blinked, then he
Shrugged and took
A royal walk . . .
NO ONE dared to
Laugh or talk.
NO ONE dared to
Say a word,
Even though
He looked absurd.

43

At last, a child,
Who didn't care
For silly rules,
Yelled,
"LOOK – HE'S BARE!"

* * * * * * * * * * * * * * * * *

Moral:
Want to seem both warm and wise?
Wear your vest – and trust your eyes.

My Unicorn

Where would you go, if you could ride a unicorn?

If I could catch a unicorn,
I'd feed him from my hand,
I'd groom him with a pearly comb
I found amongst the sand.

I'd ride him in the starlight,
Where frosty grasses gleamed,
I'd ride him under scarlet skies,
While other children dreamed.

I'd ride him to a misty wood,
And there I'd set him free –
And all the children
   in the world
Would wish
   that
   they
   were
   me.

45

Big Bad Wolf

(Little Red Riding Hood's Poem)

If you happen to meet a tall gentleman with pointy ears and enormous teeth, please don't tell him where your granny lives.

Big Bad Wolf
With your rough-scruff coat,
With your quick-flick tail
And your howl-yowl throat,
Well, you might be noisy
When you rage and roar,
And you might scare Granny
When you bang her door.

Big Bad Wolf
With your scritch-scratch claws,
With your mean-green eyes
And your snip-snap jaws,
Well, you might
be greedy
When you come to tea,
And you might scare Granny . . .
BUT YOU DON'T SCARE ME!

46

The Enchanted Porridge Pot

*I would love to use this magical porridge pot,
because it seems to make breakfast out of
NOTHING AT ALL.*

What will YOU put in the Porridge Pot?
TRUST AND TROUBLE!
Stir it cold and stir it hot
And bubble, bubble, bubble.

What will YOU put in the Porridge Pot?
DAYLIGHT AND DEW!
Stir it up and stir it down
And stew, stew, stew.

What will YOU put in the Porridge Pot?
LINGER AND LOOK!
Stir it high and stir it low
And cook, cook, cook.

What will YOU put in the Porridge Pot?
KINDNESS AND CARE!
Stir it thin and stir it thick
And share, share, share.

What will YOU put in the Porridge Pot?
WELCOME AND WISHES!
Stir it fast and stir it slow
And fill those dishes.

The Astonishingly Short Yet Exciting Story of Cinderella

*Take a deep breath before you read this poem
– then off you go . . .*

Cinders poor	–	Sweeps the floor
Work, work, work	–	Sisters smirk
Sisters whirl	–	Dresses twirl
Quick goodbyes	–	Cinders cries
Fairy sings	–	Flutters wings
Magic sprinkles	–	Cinders twinkles
Warning (one)	–	Time for fun
Coach and all	–	To the Ball
Cinders dances	–	Hero glances
Midnight, oh!	–	Scamper, go!
Cinders stumbles	–	Slipper tumbles
Home to sweep	–	Sisters sleep
Doorbell rings	–	Servant brings
Slipper! Prince!	–	Sisters wince
Cinders sits	–	Slipper fits
Wedding bells	–	Happy spells
Laughter, gold	–	Story told

Cinderella's Treasures

My most precious thing is a big book of happy photographs.

The Museum at Charming Castle is full of
    marvels . . .

A mechanical bird with a silver key;
A heap of dusty coins from a dragon's
    cave;
An invisible (but VERY expensive) suit;
A necklace made entirely from unicorn
    tears,
And, twisting like a sea-monster,
A colossal spiral of royal crowns.
(One is so small and mossy-green
We think it belonged to a frog.)

But the queue of chattering children
From the beautiful City of Ice
Would rather see Cinderella's treasures . . .

A tattered dress, as brown as a sparrow's
    feather;

A set of rusty needles and pins
Once used by the kitchen mice;
A crumbled invitation,
And, best of all

(Look, but please don't touch),

On a midnight-blue cushion
Embroidered with stars –
One glass slipper,
Slightly chipped
But still sparkling.

The Puzzled Ugly Sister

This letter was printed in the Spells R Us *magazine, but I don't know if the Fairy Godmother was able to help.*

Dear Fairy G

It's me again!
I know I look a little plain,
I know I have enormous feet
(They flip and flap along the street),
But WHY did Charming have to choose
Cinders in her see-through shoes?

It isn't right,
It isn't fair,
I ONLY want a millionaire.
I ONLY want wedding gown,
A palace and a royal crown.

So wave your wand, dear Fairy G
And find a prince for me, for me.

x x x x x x x

From

Miss Puzzled of Storyland

(PS Just in case he isn't rich,
I've also written to the Witch.)

A Letter from Puss in Boots

This letter was posted at the Storyland Post Office, and it arrived by Mouse Mail.

Dear Mr Creak of "Super Shoes"

Miaow! I bring you PAINFUL news . . .
My brand-new boots cost quite a lot,
But are they comfy? No, they're not!

They're far too high to fit a cat.
The buckles flop, the heels are flat.
The toes are tight around my paws,
So when I try to flick my claws
I make a line of little holes,
Which let in rain when thunder rolls.
And THEN the zipper traps my fur –
It pulls out tufts! I've lost my purr.

So please design some better boots,
Soft and green, the sort that suit
A handsome puss about to save
The Miller's Son (who isn't brave).

Answer quickly. Don't delay.
I fight the Ogre King TODAY!

Signed:

Puss in Boots and the Ogre King

The Miller's youngest son is very poor, but he wants to marry a princess. That means he needs a castle. And there is only one way to get it: a clever hero will have to fight the Ogre King!

"ROAR!" roared the
    Ogre King, who
    owned a lot of land.
He quickly captured
    Puss in Boots in
    one colossal hand.

"Very good," mewed
    Puss in Boots.
"You're cross and
    cruel and scary –
But I bet you can't,
    by charm or chant,
    change into something HAIRY."
Zap! went the magic. *Zim, zam, zoom!*
And there was a GRIZZLY BEAR
    growling round the room.

"Very good," mewed Puss in Boots.
"I wouldn't DARE to snigger –
But I bet you can't, by charm or chant,
    change into something BIGGER."
Bang! went the magic. *Bim, bam, boom!*
And there was an ELEPHANT stamping
    round the room.

"Very good," mewed Puss in Boots,
"You've grown a little taller –
But I bet you can't, by charm or chant,
    change into something SMALLER."
Flash! went the magic. *Flim, flam, floom!*
And there was a tiny MOUSE skipping
    round the room.

"Squeak!" squeaked the frightened
    mouse, hiding in a cup,
"Very good," yowled Puss in Boots, and
    ate the Ogre up!

The Magical Shoe Shop

*Here is another puzzle for you – I'm still
wondering about those soft fluffy shoes . . .*

What can you see through the window?

Boots for a cat,
A little glass slipper
(Whoever needs that?).
Two scarlet shoes
That skip round the shop
For ever and ever
We can't make them stop.

Small, golden trainers
For jumping downstairs
And running away
From bad-tempered bears.
Dozens of dance shoes
For naughty princesses,
Sparky black boots
To match somebody's dresses.

Massive blue wellies
For someone who strides,
The smallest of boots
For a hero who rides.
Pale satin slippers
For someone who sleeps,
Soft fluffy shoes
For a creature who creeps.

Work boots for people
Who march and who dig,
Shoes for the sisters
Whose feet are quite big.
Strong, spiky boots
For a boy who must climb . . .
Now, how many tales
Can you spot in this rhyme?

Rumpelstiltskin's Song

This is the ACTUAL song that the Jester heard in the Wild Woods.

What's my name?
What's my name?
Try three times
To win my game . . .

ONE!

Frizzy-Freddy?
Kit-kat-kong?
Naughty-Neddy?
Wrong, wrong, wrong!

TWO!

Pickle-squeezer?
Tip-tap-toe?
Sniffle-sneezer?
One last go!

THREE!

Jelly-scrumper?
Crumple-crow?
Jim-jam-jumper?
NO! NO! NO!

Can't you guess it?
What a shame . . .
RUMPELSTILTSKIN
Is my name.

The Little Goose Girl

*This story begins very sadly, but don't worry – it
all ends happily. A horrible girl steals a lucky
charm from a princess and tells lies about her.
So the nasty girl lives in a lovely palace, and the
poor princess looks after the muddy geese. Thank
goodness the truth is discovered, and after a good
wash, the princess marries a prince.*

Goose girl,
Goose girl,
Robbed by your maid,
You are a good girl,
Don't be afraid.

Goose girl,
Goose girl,
Hungry and poor,
Soon you'll have jewels,
Just as before.

Goose girl,
Goose girl,
Brave as the birds,
Breezes will spin you,
Whirling like words.

Goose girl,
Goose girl,
Sing as you run,
Magic will sparkle,
Bright as the sun.

Goose girl,
Goose girl,
Truth will grow green,
Doors will fly open –
And you'll be a queen.

Jorinda and Jorindel

*You need to know that Jorinda was a pretty
housemaid, Jorindel was a handsome gardener
and the fairy WASN'T good! The two names
sound like: Ja-RIN-da and Ja-RIN-dul.*

Jorinda and Jorindel,
They loved each other well,
Until a cruel fairy came
To cast a Birdsong Spell.

She trapped Jorinda in a cage
Of thick and thorny bars,
She turned Jorindel cold as stone
Beneath the watchful stars.

At dawn, he saw a scarlet rose,
And at its heart, a pearl.
He scattered petals round the cage –
Out flew a feathered girl!

Jorinda and Jorindel,
They live not far from YOU.
"And do you love me still?" he calls.
She sings, "I do. I do."

* *

Perhaps the fairy wasn't REALLY bad. She could have turned Jorindel into a statue, but she didn't.

A Collection of Castles

There are so many magical castles – but which one is the scariest?

Castles of glass and castles of stone.
Castles for creatures who live all alone.

Castles of dreams and castles of snow.
Castles where spiderwebs secretly grow.

Castles for ogres who FE-FI-FO-FUM.
One tiny castle for clever Tom Thumb.

Castles of ice cubes as cold as despair.
Castles that float on the warm, summer air.

Castles with turrets, castles with domes.
Old ruined castles that used to be homes.

Castles for mermaids, castles for kings.
Castles for dragons who rattle their
    wings.

Castles for dancers in rustling dresses.
Castles for princes – and happy
    princesses.

Jack's Beanstalk

If you remember the story of Jack and the Beanstalk, you'll know that he swapped his cow for a handful of beans. But what happened next?

START HERE!

Go down the vine

One Magic Bean! One Magic Spark! Here I Come Popping Out Of The Dark. Climbing And Clamber-ing, See How I Grow,

*Don't
tumble
down!*

Searching
And
Stretching
And
Scaring
A Crow.
Winding
And
Weaving
And
Waving
At Hawks,
Reaching
The
Land
Where
The
Sky
Giant
STALKS!

FINISH
HERE!

Moo! Moo!

While Jack scampered home with his magic beans
– I wonder what happened to Old Daisy the cow?

Jack was my friend   –   Me, you.
Good things must end   –   Too True.

He wore his old jeans   –   Blue, blue.
Swapped me for beans   –   Yah-boo!

A witch with a broom   –   New, new.
Whizzed to her room   –   Flew, flew.

I gloomily looked   –   Boo-hoo.
Thought I'd be cooked   –   Stew, stew.

The bubbles, the steam   – Brew, brew . . .
She just wanted cream   –   Phew, phew!

I'm loved by her cat   –   Mew, mew.
Her owl likes a chat   –   T'wit, t'woo.

I eat golden hay	–	Chew, chew.
I fly every day	–	Woo-hoo!
What do I say?	–	MOO! MOO!

Naughty Jack

Now Jack's mum has something to say – oh dear!

Naughty boy, Jack,
Swapping our cow
For beans – and a beanstalk . . .
Look at it NOW.

Naughty boy, Jack,
Climbing so high,
One day you'll tumble
And probably DIE.

Naughty boy, Jack,
Stealing a plum.
One day the Giant
Will FE-FI-FO-FUM.

Naughty boy, Jack,
Stealing his goose –
One day he'll HUFF and
Your ears will come loose.

Naughty boy, Jack,
Stealing his money.
One day he'll ROAR and
It won't seem so funny.

Naughty boy, Jack,
Stealing his harp,
One day he'll POUNCE and
His fangs will be SHARP.

Naughty boy, Jack,
Bringing home beans.
Now, stop being naughty
AND EAT UP YOUR GREENS.

* *

*Perhaps a plate of squelchy green beans was
the BEST punishment of all.*

The Frog Prince

We have a lot of frogs in our pond – but I've never tried to kiss one.

There's just a small chance that the frog
    in your pond
COULD be the prince who was bashed
    by a wand!
COULD be the hero (incredibly rich)
Cursed by the spells of a horrible witch.

Oh, hark at him croaking! How CAN
    you walk by?
His crown is so tiny, it's making me cry.
He's hopping away now. You don't want
    to miss him –
There's just a small chance you'll be
    glad . . .

IF YOU KISS HIM!

Three Fairytale Limericks

One sad dragon, one bad dragon and one surprised wolf!

There once was an ogre called Mould,
Who gave his poor Dragon a cold.
She sneezed so much smoke
She made Mouldy choke –
And then she flew off with his gold!

A witch, who thought broomsticks were
    fun,
Attempted to fly to the sun.
A dragon who spied her
Felt hungry, and fried her –
Then ATE her with chips and a bun.

There once was a wolf (bad and big)
Who wanted to bully a pig,
But before he could huff,
The wind gave a PUFF –
And now he walks round in a wig.

A Bedtime Poem

A last, sleepy poem before you turn out the
lights . . .

Close, now close the storybook.
Do not peep and do not look.
Do not try to turn the page

AND . . .

Free the Mouse King from his cage,
Comfort little Baby Bear,
Comb Rapunzel's crazy hair,
Give the ugly Beast a hug,
Leap upon a flying rug,
Visit castles far and strange,
Watch the Frog Prince glow and change,

Search for Cinderella's shoe,
Find a land where horses flew,
Trip-trap with a Billy Goat,
Sail inside a nutshell boat,
Stroke the Dragon's dreamy head . . .
Have you heard a WORD I've said?

Say goodnight to cats and queens,
Unicorns and magic beans,
Tales of joy and tales of sorrow –
Read them all again TOMORROW.

CLARE BEVAN

Fairy Poems

Do you believe in fairies?

These fairy poems were scribbled on stones and tucked under pillows, and they revealed lots of fairy secrets! In this book you will find out where the tooth fairy goes, what naughty fairies like to do for fun and how to sing fairy songs. And don't forget to practise your flying for the fairy ball!

A Bedtime Rhyme for Young Fairies

One tired fairy,
Two folded wings,
Three magic wishes,
Four daisy rings,
Five moonlight dancers,
Six starlight spells,
Seven hidden treasures,
Eight silver bells,
Nine secret doorways,
Ten keys to keep,
And one little fairy
Fast asleep.

CLARE BEVAN

Princess Poems

Could you be a princess?

A gorgeous collection of poems filled with tips on how to behave like a princess, meet the right prince and avoid the dangers posed by wicked stepmothers, dragons and unhappy fairy godmothers.

If You Were a Princess

If YOU were a princess, what would YOU ride?
A small metal dragon
with cogwheels inside?
A horse with white feathers
and hoofs of black glass?
A silvery unicorn
pounding the grass?
A fluttering carpet
that chases the bats?
A big golden pumpkin
with coachmen like rats?
A castle that sways
on an elephant's back?
A long, steamy train
going clickety clack?
Or a ship with blue sails
and YOUR name on the side?
If YOU were a princess, what would YOU ride?

CLARE BEVAN

Ballerina Poems

Do you dream of being a famous ballerina?

This book is overflowing with *graceful* and *glorious* poems about *arabesques*, ballet lessons, *glittering tutus*, ribbons, *magical music* and – gulp! – performing in a *big recital*.

The Best Bits

The best bits of ballet,
The bits that I love,
Are: my silkiest
Slippers, as soft
As a glove,
My sparkly hairgrips, my sequins
That shine, my boxes of make-up,
My ribbons that twine,
But mostly my TUTU. It's PINK.
And it's MINE!!

CLARE BEVAN

Mermaid Poems

A gorgeous collection of poems filled with glittering underwater magic!

Learn all about mermaids and their world. Watch the sea-horse races, hitch a ride on a turtle, learn mermaid names and find out about their sparkling underwater homes, their pets, the treasure they protect and the songs they sing.

What Do Mermaids Like to Wear?

What do mermaids like to wear?
Seagull feathers from the air
Twisted in their salty hair,

Bracelets made from bright blue scales,
Seaweed ribbons for their tails,
Wispy, drifty summer veils,

Glassy jewels, smooth and round,
Royal treasures (lost and found),
Shells that make a singing sound,

And snowflake stars like frozen lights,
Gathered when the ice-wind bites –
These are worn on party nights.

A selected list of titles available from Macmillan Children's Books

The prices shown below are correct at the time of going to press. However, Macmillan Publishers reserves the right to show new retail prices on covers, which may differ from those previously advertised.

Clare Bevan

Fairy Poems	978-0-330-43352-5	£4.99
More Fairy Poems	978-0-330-43935-0	£3.99
Ballerina Poems	978-0-230-01542-5	£3.99
Mermaid Poems	978-0-330-43785-2	£3.99

All Pan Macmillan titles can be ordered from our website, www.panmacmillan.com, or from your local bookshop and are also available by post from:

Bookpost, PO Box 29, Douglas, Isle of Man IM99 1BQ

Credit cards accepted. For details:
Telephone: 01624 677237
Fax: 01624 670923
Email: bookshop@enterprise.net
www.bookpost.co.uk

Free postage and packing in the United Kingdom